# NUM NUMS
## AND THE
# DESSERT
# DISASTER

SCHOLASTIC INC.
New York   Toronto   London   Auckland
Sydney   Mexico City   New Delhi   Hong Kong

ISBN 978-0-545-26231-6

12  11  10  9  8  7  6  5  4                    10  11  12  13  14  15/0

Printed in the U.S.A.    40
First printing, September 2010

Num Nums spent all day helping Patches get her garden ready for fall. After all of that hard work and fun, Num Nums was very hungry. As soon as she got home, she headed right for the kitchen and made herself a tasty treat!

Num Nums thought about how much fun she had had today and all summer long with her friends. Chunk had taught her how to surf at the beach, Scoodles had taken her exploring, and today she got to help Patches in her flower garden. She wished she could spend even more time with her amazing friends. Suddenly, Num Nums got a great idea. She should have all of her friends over for a party at her house!

Num Nums was really excited about her great idea. Seeing all of her best friends would be so much fun! She called everyone to see if they could come and they all said yes. Well, Chunk actually said, "Totally, dude," but Num Nums knew that meant "yes" coming from Chunk.

Num Nums had a lot of work to do to prepare for the party. She wanted her house to be perfect for her extra-special guests! So she got out her broom and feather duster and went to work. Soon everything in her house was tidy and clean!

Next Num Nums decided to put up some cool decorations. After all, this was a special occasion. She blew up some colorful balloons, hung some streamers, placed confetti on the tables, and even put out special napkins that said "Friends Forever" on them.

After she finished decorating her house, Num Nums needed to make treats for all of her friends to eat at the party. She thought about their favorite foods. Since Rocky and Scoodles love to explore, Num Nums decided to make them trail mix. Num Nums thought fruits and vegetables would be perfect for Jilly and Patches. And, of course, Num Nums had to make her tasty cupcakes for Mr. Squiggles and Chunk. Those were their favorite!

Num Nums got right to work making all of the food. First she mixed dried fruit and nuts together to make trail mix in a beautiful bowl that Nugget had painted for her.

Next she cut a pineapple into stars. She shaped watermelon into hearts.

For Patches, she cut extra-special tomatoes and carrots

Once she was done, she moved on to making a salad with vegetables from her garden. Last, she put in her favorite vegetable, carrots. While she was chopping them up, Num Nums ate a few—she just couldn't help herself!

Next Num Nums moved on to baking her cupcakes. She mixed all of the ingredients together and poured the batter into the cupcake tins. Then she put them in the oven to bake. She couldn't wait to decorate them with her cool pink icing and purple sprinkles!

After all of that hard work, Num Nums certainly was tired. She could smell the delicious cupcakes baking. All she had to do was clean up her kitchen. But first she thought she would rest her eyes for just a moment. After all, she had worked very hard all day and deserved a five-minute nap. So she lay down and closed her eyes.

Soon Num Nums was fast asleep. She dreamed about all of her friends having fun at her fabulous party. She dreamed about eating cupcakes, but when she got near them, they smelled like smoke! That woke Num Nums right up. *Oh no!* She had forgotten about her cupcakes baking in the oven!

Num Nums ran over to the oven as fast as she could, forgetting about her fruit, salad, and trail mix on the table. When she turned the corner, she slipped and knocked over her bowls full of food! When Num Nums finally pulled herself up from her fall, she went over to the oven. It no longer smelled delicious. The cupcakes were ruined! They looked like black rocks!

Everything was a mess! The cupcakes were burnt to a crisp, all of the other treats had spilled onto the floor, and her kitchen was dirty. She didn't have enough time to clean up, go to the store to buy all of the ingredients, and then remake all of the treats. Her party was ruined!

Num Nums felt like crying. All of her friends were looking forward to the party and her delicious food! She couldn't disappoint them— she would just have to cancel the party. She would have to call them after she cleaned up. Just then, the doorbell rang. *Oh no,* Num Nums thought, *my friends are here already!* She hadn't realized how late it was.

21

When she opened the door, it was Mr. Squiggles. He was a little early.

"Hi, Mr. Squiggles," Num Nums said, trying not to cry.

"What's wrong, Num Nums?" Mr. Squiggles asked. He could tell right away that his friend was very upset.

"I have to cancel the party," she replied.

"But why?" Mr. Squiggles asked. "Everyone is looking forward to seeing their friends."

"I know, and I feel terrible, but I've ruined all of the food and just don't have enough time to make everything all over again," Num Nums said with tears in her eyes.

"Well, can I at least help you clean up and keep you company?" Mr. Squiggles asked.

"No, that's all right. I made the mess, so I will clean it up. But you could do me a favor and let everyone else know the party is canceled," she said.

"Sure," Mr. Squiggles answered.

As Mr. Squiggles left Num Nums' house, he ran right into the rest of their friends. Everyone had been on their way to the party. They were all very disappointed to learn it had been canceled!

"I feel so bad for Num Nums—she did all that hard work and now there is no party!" Chunk said.

"Yeah, poor Num Nums!" Jilly agreed.

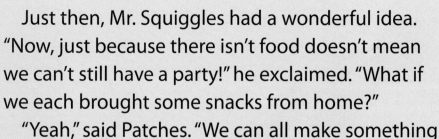

Just then, Mr. Squiggles had a wonderful idea. "Now, just because there isn't food doesn't mean we can't still have a party!" he exclaimed. "What if we each brought some snacks from home?"

"Yeah," said Patches. "We can all make something quick and easy. Let's meet back here in an hour to surprise Num Nums!"

The party wasn't ruined after all!

Num Nums was feeling pretty down in the dumps. She couldn't believe she had ruined her special party! She cleaned up the whole kitchen. Then she started to take down the decorations. Just then, she heard a knock at her door. *Who could that be?* she thought.

Num Nums hurried to open the door. All of her friends were waiting on her front porch!

"Surprise!" everyone yelled.

"What are you all doing here?" Num Nums asked. She was definitely surprised.

"We couldn't let you cancel the party after all of your hard work, so we decided to surprise you!" Mr. Squiggles said.

"We each made a special treat!" Jilly explained. "So there is plenty of food for the party!"

"I hope you like carrot cake!" Patches added.

"Squeak, squeaky squeak squeak squeaker squeakiest, squeaky squeak!" Pipsqueak chimed in.

"She's right." Scoodles nodded. "She said we were excited to come have a party with you, not to eat food."

Once everyone came inside, Num Nums looked around the room at all of her amazing friends. She was so happy that everyone had come over and surprised her. Everyone was having a blast hanging out and talking about all of the fun things they had done that summer. She couldn't believe she had tried to cancel the party just because of one little mistake! She really was lucky to have such thoughtful friends.

Everyone had an amazing time at the party and decided to try to have a special friendship party again next weekend.

"Only this time," Mr. Squiggles said, "no napping while you are baking!"

Num Nums laughed along with all of her friends. It had been the perfect party after all.